BROKEN FOREVER

Amadi Arua

Flower Press
Montreal, Canada

ISBN-13: 978-0-9877632-5-9

BROKEN FOREVER

This book is a work of fiction. Names, characters, places and incidents either are products of the author's imagination or are used fictitiously. Any resemblance to actual events or locales or persons, living or dead, is entirely coincidental.

Published by Flower Press
Montreal, Canada

www.FlowerPress.ca

To elder Sunday Ukwuoma Ochu
and Hajiah Habiba Mary Ochu

1

THE wind was strong grumbling and rumbling as it swept violently across the city of Moscow. The sun had now gone, hiding itself perfectly behind the cloud when Dima Kisa got home.

After some minutes the wind stopped, above in the sky was the moon. After having his meal, he walked out to one of the house's verandas to relax sitting on the chair. Soon the wind began again.

Dry leaves rustled endlessly providing a rhythmic atmosphere as they danced, scratching the earth's surface and rolling to where the wind pointed, rather unwillingly. Rapidly the moon remained full as it brightened the night, soon the moon began to withdraw gradually into the thick dark cloud. Visibility became reduced under the harsh weather except through the help of electricity. Lightening flashed severally, followed by the booming thunder and just then the rain came fast and then slanting showers.

Dima Kisa stood up from where he was relaxing, stretched himself and strolled into the house obviously to retire and to sleep. He sat on the bed and cast a vacant gaze into the darkroom.

He closed his eyes, took a deep breath and then he said his prayers silently.

Soon he snoozed off.

The telephone rang. It was about the ninth consecutive time yet it had not been answered. Dima Kisa felt disturbed by the persistent ringing of the telephone which was gradually turning into a nuisance.

"God why should somebody wake up by the intent of disturbing others at odd hours like this?" he asked himself as he rolled his massive frame restlessly all over the giant size bed. This was definitely not the best time to wake him from his sleep with a telephone call. He treasured it so much especially after a hard day's job coupled with his usual series of night meetings.

The phone rang again and again.

Dima Kisa got up, stretched himself and staggered into the rest room, returned later and threw himself back into the bed. The caller persisted and the telephone continued to ring ceaselessly. Dima Kisa had hoped that the caller would become tired and give up eventually. Reluctantly he reached for the receiver and spoke.

"Hello… who is this bed bug?" his voice was cold and his eyes were still weak.

"It's me Dimitry Misha, just want to remind you of our meeting with you tomorrow in the morning at our usual meeting place."

Dima Kisa hissed and banged the phone and slept off again like a baby.

Hours rolled by and soon it was morning.

Dima Kisa walked majestically into the lavishly furnished reception of the Olympic hotel, looking cute in a brilliantly designed black colored suit. His roving eyes caught a smartly dressed lady receptionist busy attending to customers. After some inquiries, he took the elevator to room 419. Gently he knocked on the door and pushed it open immediately without waiting for any response.

He strolled in, closed the door quietly behind him and tactfully cast a gaze into the dimly lit room and recognized three men who sat at a small table at the far left corner.

In the middle was Dimitry Misha, a cop chief. On his left sat Valodic Ivan, the boss of the immigration department. Maxism Invanova sat at the back. He was a top naval officer, noted for his wide spread connections within and outside the country. Dima Kisa gave out a toothy smile exposing a set of teeth badly stained by tobacco and hard drugs as he walked towards the men.

Everywhere was calm, Dima Kisa exchanged greetings with the men and then sat on the only vacant seat left. He lit a cigar, sucked it hard and released thick and dirty white clouds of smoke. Gradually he lifted a bag, placed it on the table and unzipped it, revealing bundles of hundred dollars. Maxism Ivanova drew his seat closer as if doubtful of what caught his eyes. His eye balls grew larger as if they would jump out of their sockets. Dimitry Misha and Valodia Ivan were also surprised and wore expressions that seemed to ask where did this man get all this money from.

The men looked at each other at Dima Kisa and then back at themselves. No doubt Dima Kisa was now expected to break the sudden silence that had engulfed the room, but he pretended to be absent minded. Instead he took another long puff of his cigar and polluted the room with more smoke. Soon he got up, paced up and down and later returned to the table. He drew out his seat and sat more comfortably by crossing his legs.

"Gentlemen you are all aware that all of us are into this deal together, but with the recent catch of my men I am not happy. I will not want this to repeat again this is why I have decided to come and see you… I am doing my best to make sure my boys who were arrested by the cops regain their freedom again through the court that is it…!" he spoke with a fixed gaze at the men, his eyes were red like the tongues of fire. They looked like a sharp sword that could pierce ones loin and hurt so badly. "First a deal is struck. The business begins and next the proceeds start flowing," he added.

Dimitry Misha nodded and smiled.

"You mean all this comes from our last business that coursed the arrest of your boys?" Valodia Ivan asked.

"Yes," Dima Kisa replied. "Just one deal… just one deal,"

he added.

There was silence.

"We could even make more money, if only..." Dima Kisa said and paused to gauge their pulse and then continued. "All I need is your cooperation. It is a very lucrative business, desired by many, but only a few people can do it successfully."

"Exactly..."

"You are indeed privileged to be part of it," Dima Kisa interrupted Valodia Ivan. "Crude oil is the diamond from the developing world and girls mean money these days... real money, but none enriches people like drugs. Now before we share the money I must remind you the rules of the game once more. All I need is your cooperation."

The men listened attentively.

"As we eat and drink together the drug business proceeds and we will go down together, if it is needed."

"Never, we will keep on assuring you our protection," Dimitry Misha said.

The men shared the money and soon began heading to their various homes.

"Do we meet here in the evening?" asked Dimitry Misha looking at Dima Kisa.

"What for?" he replied.

"Just for a brief talk concerning our business..."

"No! I don't have time. Whenever I want us to meet I will always tell you through my contact people."

"Dima Kisa listen to me, I want to have a talk with you at the Sedimoi continent hotel. There is an investigation going on right now and I want to give you the whole details and those detectives that are involved, but that will be after the in house course on investigation and investigation techniques to trap you down."

"Really?" Dima Kisa asked.

"Yes Pushkin is going to be the lecturer. Remember he is the senior staff of the Bureau of the Drug Peddlers Investigations, the BDPI." Dimitry Misha said.

Dima kisa nodded "Then when can we fix the next meeting?"

"By noon today…"

"No!" Dima Kisa interrupted. "It will not be possible. By noon I have a bank transaction. Why not we meet at the Volgino club?"

"When?" Dimistry Misha asked.

"Tonight I will be there…"

"No I will not be out tonight. I have a discussion with my wife. Well I will tell you when we will meet next time," Dimitry Misha said.

"Alright." Dima Kisa replied and they parted.

2

THE security men in the investigation unit listened attentively as Pushkin delivers his lecture on investigation and investigation techniques.

"Like I have told you earlier that investigation and the act of mastering its various techniques is one of the most important and vital tools in any security circle for investigation to be successfully be it criminal or noncriminal investigations, its conducts must involve several phases of receipt and verification of information as well as planning that is necessary to develop the case," Pushkin said and began to walk around in the classroom.

A woman that sat right in front of him nodded. She was one of the senior cop officers in the class, the only female one and she was a lawyer too.

"This in house course would attempt to define and discuss the concept of investigations, aim of investigations, types of investigations, principles of investigations, qualities expected of an investigator and lastly the various techniques of investigation. However, in the outline of the various techniques of investigation, I would try to be as brief as possible as each technique is a topic of its own. Am I well understood?" Pushkin asked.

"Yes sir," the cops responded.

"So it is expected that at the end of this in house course, officers especially those from the headquarter would be able to appreciate the value and strength of investigations as its affects our jobs bearing at the back of our minds that the success or failure of any cop operations could largely be or depend on the proper or improper conduct of investigations?" asked corporal Romanov.

"Yes you are right," Pushkin replied.

There was silence.

"What is investigation?" the lecturer asked.

"The Merriam Webster's collegiate dictionary of English 10th edition defines investigation as to observe or study by close observation and systematic enquiry, to make a systematic examination and to conduct an official enquiry," Maxism Ivanova, a male cop sitting on the right side beside the only female cop in the class said.

The lecturer nodded.

"The advanced learners dictionary also define investigate as follows: find out and examine all the facts about a case in order to obtain the truth," Dimitry Misha another male cop sitting on the left side beside the female cop in the class added.

"Based on what the two officers in this class have said, it's now very clear that investigation can be defined as the carrying out of a systematic inquiry into a matter. It is basically evident in its function. It can also be said to be a process of gathering information and making inquiry with a view to achieve results.

Therefore, in the context of narcotic investigations and investigations can then be defined further as the systematic process of acquiring information through inquiry or otherwise with a view to determine the degree and magnitude of involvement of a person or group of people in a drug related case or in other words to identify guilty people in a drug related case," said the lecturer as he stared at the man seated at the last row.

"You, as an officer for this unit what are the aims or goals of investigation?"

"Basically every investigation be it criminal or noncriminal is aimed at accomplishing three main objectives namely: identify the guilty person, to locate a person and identify his haunts and lastly, provide evidence against a person," said Romanov.

"Class is that right?" the lecturer asked.

"Yes sir," they replied.

"Just like we have in the aims or goals of investigations are three main objectives. There are two main types of investigations and these are: criminal investigation and non criminal investigation. Who can tell us what criminal investigations are involved?" the lecturer asked.

"Narcotic investigation, financial crime investigation, assets investigation, arson, sabotage, theft, subversion, fraud, forensic homicide and many of criminals." corporal Romanov explained.

The lecturer nodded.

"While non criminal investigation include: medical, journalistic and scientific investigation," Romanov added. The lawyer cop turned back from her seat to have a look at the man who gave the answer. She wore dark glasses and looked unfriendly.

"Thank you Romanov, I am glad you have a good understanding of the types of investigations we have," the lecturer said.

"Thank you sir," Romanov replied.

"Now I want to tell you about the principles of investigation," the lecturer said. "You see the basic principles of investigations are divided into three and the first is that it must be centrally controlled, it must be objective, the informants and sources of information must be properly exploited and protected. Lastly investigation must be conducted with clearly defined goals, so as to avoid discrepancies that can hinder conclusions. Do you have any questions?"

Nobody said a word.

"With your silence, it is assumed that I am well understood," said the lecturer.

"Yes sir," the cops replied.

The lecturer walked to the blackboard and wrote, "The qualities of an investigator," he turned and faced the cops in the class. "What are the qualities a good and sound investigator must be able to possess?" he asked.

"He must be able to establish a good reputation for ethical conduct in developing successful cases. And he must have a keen insight in human nature and motivation," the female cop said.

"Exactly," the lecturer replied.

"He must have familiarity with areas of activities in which he is involved and he must have familiarity with the identities and behaviors of people living and working in areas of his responsibility," said Romanov, in a calm tone.

The lecturer nodded.

"He must be skilled in interviewing, also must be hardworking and must be a painstaking worker. He must be loyal, honest and have of high integrity. Lastly he must have a good level of intellect, be able to think fast so as to have the ability to pre empt an enemy situation," said Dimitry Misha.

"That's right," muttered the lecturer.

"He must have a quickness of mind in decision making, should be able to discriminate or distinguish between relevant and irrelevant things and make judgement. He must not be a double agent, he must be flexible, adoptable and have a keen sense of observation," Valodia Ivan said.

The lecturer licked his lips.

"He must have a stable character, he must not be paranoid, psychotic or neurotic. He must have appreciation of the true value of information received," Maxism Ivanova said.

I am glad that we all in this class know what qualities are expected of an investigator to have to make him or her a good and sound investigator," the lecturer added.

There was silence.

"Do we continue or go on break?"

"Continue sir," the security man responded.

Pushkin smiled and continued, "as you can see there is trouble in Russia caused by drug barons and peddlers so to say. The success over peddlers cannot be achieved alone by one group of a security agent. We must be all involved in the investigation techniques and we must all work in partnership to achieve success. As you can see this is why we have invited the naval staffs and the immigration for this course because both are very relevant in the success of this very fight to cut down drug barons in Russia."

"Sir is it true that the suspected Dima Kisa escaped his arrest some months ago when the cops stormed the peddlers environment?" asked one cop in the class.

"Yes he did, but he is still wanted…"

"He can't be a wanted person when he is walking freely in Moscow sir," another person interrupted the lecturer.

"There is a lack of evidence against him and so we are helpless and cannot get him arrested at all. Once we are able to get enough proof then we will trap him down. To get him trapped down that is why we are in this class learning the best step to catch him and his informants," the lecturer said.

Those in the class were excited.

"For drug or narcotic investigation to be fully successful, its conduct must be involved in several phases which include the receipt and verification of information, as well as the planning that is necessary to properly develop the case in question. Some of the common investigative techniques that are usually put to use includes: searches, surveillance, elicitation, interview, interrogation, statement taking, court and other things. What I want you to understand is that each investigative technique I have mentioned is a topic on its own, but for the purpose of this in house training course, I will only attempt to define and discuss these topics one by one, but in a nutshell and at the day it is expected that you would be able to appreciate and assimilate the various points I have enumerated putting into great cognizance how each play a key or vital role in various processes of investigation," said the lecturer and looking at the security men in the class.

The security men listened attentively.

"We have to begin with the searches. To search is to look into over carefully and thoroughly in an effort to finally discover something. In another words to look and explore by inspecting possible places and modes of concealment. One of the duties of a cop officer is to conduct searches or the supervision of other officers in a search. The aim or essence of every search is to discover one or more search reasons which includes, to locate hidden exhibit such as hard drugs," the lecturer said.

The lawyer nodded.

"To discover documents that may link the suspect and or any other person with drug trafficking. To collect materials that may be used against the suspect if and when the case is charged to court. To check the reliability of informants and lastly to check the commission of a crime," the lecturer added. "From these reasons, it is crystal clear that searching is one of the most important techniques of true investigation is that not true?"

"It is," they responded.

"You, what is surveillance?" the lecturer asked pointing at Valodia Ivan.

"Surveillance can be defined as the secretive, continuous and sometimes periodic watching of people, cars, places or objects to obtain information concerning the activities and identities of individuals. Surveillance is often the only investigative technique available to identify sources, couriers and recipient of drugs, hideouts and accomplices," Valodia Ivan said.

Everybody listened attentively.

"The goal and objectives of surveillance is to obtain evidence of a crime, to protect undercover officers or to colaborate their testimony. To locate people by watching their haunts and associates check in the reliability of informants. To prevent the commission of a crime, to apprehend a suspect during the commission of a crime and to obtain information for later use during interrogation. To develop leads on information received from other sources. It can be used to provide protection for very important people from my explanation, my various reasons and goals are outlined. It is also crystal clear that surveillance is one of the major techniques of hinvestigation," Valodia Ivan added.

"You are right I love that." the lecturer replied pointing at Dimitry Misha. "In investigation and investigation techniques what is elicitation?"

"Well, elicitation can be defined as the acquiring of information by the way of interaction with a target person as the suspect without the person knowing about it. The information is actually acquired through conversation without the suspect being aware that he is being exploited. In eliciting for information, it is important to note that the subject should not be allowed to know one's real interest in having the conversation. Information can be elicited during social gatherings such as parties, ceremonies, clubbing and a lot of others," said Dimitry Misha.

The lecturer nodded.

"Elicitation is often used when the information that is required is what can be picked up through casual conversation with the subject and there is no need to institute the elaborate interview and interrogation techniques. In cases where the information required from the subject is not forth coming then it may become necessary to arrange for a formal interview and to conduct an interrogation," Dimitry Misha nodded.

"Why does the elicitation work?" the lecturer asked.

"It works because people like to talk about themselves especially to good listeners. Most people are susceptible to flattery especially when it is done in a subtle manner and lastly it works because people like to be listened to especially if they have an idea or believe in a cause," said Dimitry Misha.

"Thank you." the lecturer replied.

"Sir I want to talk about the interview," Maxism Ivanova said, looking at the lecturer.

"Alright go ahead," replied the lecturer.

"This can be defined as the process of questioning and examining a source or a targeted person in order to obtain information that is important for better understanding the fact of a matter.

It is the primary way of obtaining information from people who by virtue of their closeness to or involvement in or awareness of a situation or their interaction over the years have personal or exclusive knowledge of important facts of a case. An interview also is supposed to be a two way affair example, one person asking the questioning while the other person who is normally the subject answering the question. It is a formal conversation conducted for the purpose of obtaining information. An interview may involve virtually witnesses, informants, citizens and depending on the type of investigation and the suspect. As a general rule suspects under investigation are not interviewed, but rather they are interrogated. An interview can evolve or metamorphosed to an interrogation. A person being interviewed is not under compulsion to answer questions put to him by the interviewer as he has the fundamental rights of whether to answer questions or not," Maxism Ivanova explained.

"Are you aware that there are basically four different types of interviews?" the lecturer asked.

"Yes sir," replied Maxism Ivanova. "We have employment interview, promotion interview, opinion pole or survey and investigative interviews. This is the type of interview that will interest any security operative and by extension. This type of interview is conducted to unravel the facts of a case under investigations."

"Now let us talk about the principles of the interview," said the lecturer. All interviews must be guided by principle which in return helps the officer interviewing the interviewee to achieve maximum success. The principles of the interview are divided into four. The first is called the definitive purpose. What did I call it?"

"Definitive purpose," they all responded.

"The reason for the interview must be clearly spelled out or must be well defined which should form the basis of the interview," the lecturer said.

The female lawyer nodded.

"We have the initiative. In this case the officer interviewing should exercise the position of authority over the subject being interviewed.

You see the position of authority is lost if the subject becomes angry over the interviewer's arrogance. Also the position of authority is lost if the interviewer allows the interviewee to create confusion. Am I understood?"

"Yes sir," they all replied.

"The next is accuracy. The interviewer must be accurate, have doubts, repeat questions and report correctly thereafter. The last is called the use of force. In this case, force, threats, mental torture, insults and whatever you may think of must not be used in the conduct of an interview. Any questions?"

"No questions sir," the people replied.

"You, I want you to tell us what you have understood by the word interrogation as it relates to investigation and investigation techniques?" the lecturer said pointing at the female lawyer.

"Interrogation can be defined as the systematic questioning of a person for the purpose determining the level of involvement of the person in a crime. In other words interrogation is the questioning of a suspect under investigation. It should not be confused with elicitation or interview because in elicitation or interview the subject is not aware that the information is being extracted from him while in the interview the subject is aware that he is being questioned, but also know that he is not completely or absolutely under the control of the person questioning him." the lady cop said. "Since interrogation is the questioning of a suspect whose fundamental rights to freedom of movement has been withdrawn.

These people are suspects under custody the same principles that apply at the interview are also applicable in interrogation," she added.

There was silence.

Then the lady continued, "there are basically different types of interrogation techniques and the selection of one approach depends on the circumstances of a case and the suspects personality. These approaches include the logical approach, the sympathetic and friendly approach, the aggressive and hostile approach, the good and bad approach, egotistical approach, the exaggeration approach, I know it all approach and the rapid fire approach."

"I love your explanation thank you," said the lecturer, looking right into the lady's eyes.

"Thank you very much," the lady said.

"Lastly we are going to look into the statement," the lecturer said. "A statement is a written record of an occurrence usually by a person containing the details of a person that has to say about the occurrence. The statement should always be made as soon as possible that is when the story is still fresh. We have two types of statements are you aware of this?"

"Yes sir," the security officers responded.

"The first is called the statement of a suspect of witness," said a male naval staff. "The statement of a suspect is what an accused person has written or a record of what the suspect has to say about a given allegation. It could be confessional, denial or there is no statement. It must begin at the top with cautionary words," he added.

"I love that," the lecturer said. "You see when we are talking about a confessional statement, it is an admittance of a person or suspect that the person has committed the crime in question. You, what is a denial statement?" he asked and pointed at Romanov.

"It is a written record by a person disagreeing, denying or refusing to accept the allegation of committing a crime in question," Romanov explained.

The lecturer nodded.

Romanov continued, "When we talk about no statement this is also a written record in this case the suspect may insist that he will not make any statement or he may wish to give conditions as to how he will give statement or even state categorically that he will not make any. The investigator would simply request the suspect to write on the statement sheet that he does not want to make any statement."

"Thank you my dear," the lecturer said. "In conclusion to all we have been talking I wish to state that it is my belief that this lecture has succeeded in throwing or shading more light into what investigation is all about and the various techniques of investigation," the lecturer added.

There was silence.

"Thank you ladies and gentlemen." said the lecturer.

"Thank you too," they all replied.

The lecture ended and everybody parted from the class. The lady cop was walking back to her office when Mr. Benson approached her and exchanged greetings.

"I am going to assign you to work with Pushkin in getting the drug barons in our society arrested. You are going to use a forged name."

"What is it?" Jane asked.

"Masha Alexy Nketia." Mr. Benson replied.

Jane listened attentively.

"Going by this name, you have to apply seductive investigation and investigation techniques to your work. All I need is results, I want Dima Kisa trapped down. You have to go in disguise that will change your face, voice and clothes.

You have to subject yourself to a fake and artificial life. This time next month come to my office for a letter you will give to Pushkin. I will provide disguises and funds to enable you effectively carry out the assigned duty." said Mr. Benson.

"But I thought Pushkin and corporal Romanov are on the project already?"

"They are, but you have a bigger role to play and they have to be successful."

"It is alright, I will do that once I am assigned for the job." Jane said. Mr. Benson thanked her for accepting the project.

Two weeks later, as the day was Monday.

Pushkin was busy packing files into his office cabinet when Mr. Benson the cop boss walked in. Quickly Pushkin stopped all he was doing to attend to his boss.

"Good day sir," Pushkin said.

"Thank you Pushkin," the boss replied. "Well I am carrying out an office inspection that is why I am here," the cop boss said.

Pushkin listened attentively.

"I have gotten a report on the lecture you had for the security men two weeks ago and I am highly impressed because it is the talk of the whole Moscow."

"Really?" Pushkin asked.

"Yes," the boss replied.

Pushkin was very glad.

Next week the high court judge will be deciding if those caught by the cops are guilty or not, but that will not discourage us. Eventually the suspects are not found guilty of our charges against them we will keep on fighting. One thing is certain Dima Kisa is a peddler and we have to apply every investigation and investigation techniques to get him trapped down. Do you hear me?" the boss asked.

"Yes I do," Pushkin responded.

"I will have more talks on the phone with you concerning how to get Dima Kisa trapped down. I will also arrange for those who will help you to work out your plans so that at the end we will get him red handed. Do you hear me?"

"Yes sir," Pushkin said.

The boss was glad, he commented on that Pushkin efforts again before he walked away.

3

IN Russia, Yakutua was a city closest to China. It's a beautiful place any decent person would like to go there when they visit Russia. One Monday morning in 1988 the atmosphere of Yakutia suddenly changed. It was electric with a sea of heads at the court premises. Many had anticipated the situation and had left their homes to secure vantage positions to witness the historic verdict of a case that had dragged for months. Newspaper vendors made soaring sales at the court premises as people struggled to buy copies of the newspapers. Most of them carried stories on the case. The banner headlines were alluring and some of them in colors.

At exactly 7:45 am a Mercedes Benz filled with cops drove furiously into Yakutia city court premises. They had come to beef up security and to ensure that the surging crowd was put in check. The Russian Democratic government's had a lot to deal with at stake. The government saw the intricate case as an opportunity to redeem its battered status among the community of nations occasioned by peddlers.

The government ensured tight security at the trial venue and hoped that justice would prevail and a sentence the court will pass will be acceptable to the international jury.

Soon the door to the court room swung open. The security men with metal detectors searched everybody that struggled to gain entrance, including accredited journalists and press photographers, who had come from local and international media organizations before letting them in. After a while, the court room was filled to capacity as people took up every available space. Some of them sat on the bare floor and the security men ordered those who could not be accommodated in the heated up room to stay outside. It was seven minutes to nine o'clock. The crowd murmured and whispered as they glued their eyes to the court's entrance gate with the anxiety boldly written on their faces.

Suddenly a Mercedes Benz Black Maria was soon spotted approaching the court entrance and the crowd went wild. They squealed and shouted. The eight notorious suspects peddlers alighted from the Black Maria, dressed in beautiful clothes, clean, shaven and healthy looking. This was an evidence that they were being well looked after by the Russian prison authorities. People jumped, stood on the tip of their toes shoved and pushed, just to have a glimpse of the men that had held the Russian country to ransom with their criminality. Those outside, climbed the fence, cars, trees and for a good look at the rascal peddlers whose activities have sent many cops to their untimely death in their efforts to get them arrested.

A young costume shop owner said to the lady beside him, "I just wish the leader of the gang is caught."

"You mean their leader escaped?" the lady asked.

"Yes!" the man replied, he now saw the faces of the eight suspects clearly and waved at them, victoriously. "In the cause of getting them arrested it was a great battle between them and the cops. Many of them lost their lives to the cops bullets and also many cops lost theirs too to the peddlers bullets."

The lady listened attentively.

"What the fight caused was a creation of an opportunity for Dima Kisa to escape for safety and his faceless informant whom we heard is a cop," the man added.

"You mean Dima Kisa is a peddler?"

"So we heard, but nobody is too sure. They caught peddlers claimed that he is not part of them, but the cop report show that he is a suspect though they don't have gotten strong proof to their claims that is why they have allowed him to walk about still as a free man."

The lady heaved a sigh.

Just then the judge walked in and took his seat. He stared at the eight suspects and immediately turned his eyes to the documents before him. In a mono tone, he read out the names of the suspects. He calmly surveyed the over crowded court room and without any emotion in his voice said, "You all have been sentenced to death. You will be hanged. May God have mercy on your souls."

The crowd went wild with jubilation. Many members of a non government organization that is into war against illicit drug business could not contain their joy as they marched around the court premises with the Russian flags raised high in the air. They danced and sang varying choruses, many times over around the court premises before surging to the cop's office in Yakutia. The left over crowd in the court premises soon began to disperse in small groups to different direction and discussed the sentence.

"Please young man, I understand that you know Dima Kisa too well. My name is Natasha and he wants me to be his girl friend. He has promised to be doing all my wishes for me. I want to know him too well before responding to his request. Will you help me to achieve that?" the lady asked.

"Providing you will not implicate him."

"I will not! What is your name?"

"I am Zhena," he replied and told her all about himself. Natasha did the same. They exchanged contacts and agreed to become close friends. Both of them were very glad.

Two weeks later. It was Monday.

At the cop headquarters. The cops were all very busy walking to and from the office premises. Everybody was very busy at his or her work. Soon the telephone in Pushkin's office rang and nobody picked up the receiver.

The telephone rang again. It was about the third consecutive time now yet it had not been answered. Detective superintendent Pushkin felt disturbed by the persistent ringing of the telephone, which was gradually turning into a nuisance. He was in his office going through reports in a file sent at his table from Mr. Benson's office. Pushkin had hoped that the caller would become tired and give up eventually, but instead it continued. Reluctantly, he reached for the receiver and spoke.

"Hello… who is on the line?" his voice was calm.

"It is Mr. Benson... I hope you have gotten the file I sent to you?" the voice replied.

"Yes sir! Right now I am on it."

"That's alright… one of the senior female cop officers who is a lawyer will be working with you starting from tomorrow."

"What is her name sir?" Pushkin asked.

"She will introduce herself to you when she comes to your office. I will give her the letter and she will hand it over to you. Trust her and make sure you work in partnership with her. Do you hear me well?"

"Yes sir!" Pushkin replied.

"Are you aware that Dima Kisa has left Yakutia city to Moscow?"

"I just received the signal about half an hour ago. I equally was informed that cops in Yakutia have all been transferred to various cop stations in Russia and new cops from other stations posted to Yakutia city to take over their duty post. And I think your action was right…"

"You see, in Yakutia, there are bad eggs among the cops who have been linked men to the suspected peddler making him to always jump our traps that was why I directed that the cops should all be posted out," Mr. Benson interrupted.

"It's a good idea sir!"

"So you are to lead the investigation team on the activities of the peddlers and report directly to me. I want result no matter what it is going to take you. Also find out among the cops in Moscow whose name is Kolia because the report says, he is the one that feeds the peddlers with information on our operational styles."

"There is no name like that sir. All I know is that among the cops, Dima Kisa has one who is his in law suspected to be a corrupt cop though not yet proved," Pushkin said.

"Good! I like that information. Now you have to equally monitor the movement and activities of the cop he may be this mysterious Kolia among the cops… see what you can do to have access to all Dima Kisa's bank transactions."

"But you know that the banks don't disclose the finances of their customers, what am I to do so is to get contact with his bank account because it's very good I have the information." Pushkin interrupted.

"In one hour, I will give a directive to the bank manager through the central bank authorizing you and your female partner in the investigation to have access to Dima Kisa's accounts and daily bank transactions. Do you hear me?"

"Yes sir!" Pushkin replied.

"But you have to keep this very secret."

"I will do that." Pushkin replied.

"The mysterious Kolia in your midst is disguised that is another report right on my table and I want you to use any cop you feel that sounds good and useful to your field of work to unmask the masked cop. Good luck Pushkin."

"Thank you sir," Pushkin replied. He put the receiver down and went deep in thought wondering how to carry out the assignment.

4

MANY months later it was a beautiful morning. The sun was at its best shining with grandeur littering shadows of men, women and objects everywhere. The streets in Moscow were busy as usual with hustling and bustling at its crest. The day's struggle usually started before day break and thickened with sunset each day including Sundays. Often times visitors went home with various tales about Moscow. Some said people hardly slept while others had stories that it was the city that actually never slept. Whatever they felt they spoke freely, but the situation remained the same.

This morning was a perfect picture of what life in the city of Moscow looked like. People and businesses were on the move. People walking long and short distances, riding in cars, on motor bikes and boarding taxis.

Mekloho Maklaya street has a bee hive of activities. Like a swam of bees, people and mostly businesses, busied the street. It was 11:45am, detective Pushkin drove in his new car with corporal Romanov and parked in front of the bank at the Kwame

Nkrumah area at Moscow.

The bureau of the drug peddlers investigations is the criminal detection department of the cops. It is a special elite force that works quietly, but effectively to protect Russians.

Pushkin idly toyed with what he would do if all the money in the bank building was given to him. He shook his head regretfully. That could never happen. But there was no harm in entertaining that idea.

He looked at the young corporal Romanov, who was sitting beside him on the passenger seat of the car and called him playfully, "corporal, what would you do if all the money in this bank was given to you?"

Corporal Romanov laughed out and replied respectfully, "Sir, I think the first thing I will do is to faint. And when I recover my senses, I will just pack all my things, leave this terrible city of Moscow and go straight back to my home at the country side."

Pushkin looked at the young officer in curiosity. "What would you be doing with all that money in your small home at the country side?"

"With all due respects to you sir, I will just go to the home and think up a thousand and one ways to spend all that money without working for the rest of my life. And I will begin by marrying forty wives."

This time, Pushkin laughed out loud with his junior officer. He was about to say something else when the middle aged man he had been expecting emerged out of the glass doors of the bank. Pushkin sat up well in his seat and looked carefully through his wind screen at the man who had come out of the bank. Corporal Romanov's eyes followed that of his boss. Romanov was to see a man of about fifty years old with a thick stick of cigar in his mouth. The cigar was unlit, but one could tell he had not lighted it only in deference to the fact that he had just emerged out of the bank which is a public place.

The man with the unlit cigar was expensively dressed in some very nice imported suit and handmade Italian crocodile shoes.

The texture of his skin told of a man who had been enjoying immense wealth for a very long time of his life. On his head was a soft felt hat and his movements spoke of a man who knew with a lot of worldly wisdom. He was not the type of man you could fool easily. More likely, he would be the one to fool you.

Behind him walked a heavily muscled macho man who held his brief case. It was clear that the man in the hat had either gone to withdraw some money from the bank or deposit some. Whatever transactions he may have gone to the bank to conduct would involve some huge amount. That explained the presence of the macho bodyguard.

The two striking men walked to a Mercedes Benz E500. All eyes turned to watch them and a secret smile escaped the lips of the man with the felt hat. It was evident that he was enjoying the immense attention he was attracting.

The macho bodyguard promptly opened the back door for his boss and when they later had sat down, he himself went behind the driving wheel and eased the car into gear on drive and drove the car towards Moscow Central.

Corporal Romanov whistled softly after the expensive car had glided away. "What a car!"

Pushkin gestured with his head at the departing car. "That German car must worth about $250,000.

"All that for a single car?" the junior officer asked. "I swear some Russians are rich!"

Pushkin refrained from commenting on the wealth of Russians and instead asked, "Do you know that man, Romanov?"

"No sir," the corporal replied. "But I wouldn't mind being his friend. Especially with all that money he must by all means have."

"Well," Pushkin replied. "That man is the object of our surveillance at this bank. Valadia Oleg alias Dima Kisa styles himself as an international business man who deals with oil products. But we all know the kind of business he deals on. Unfortunately he is so smart and covers his business activities so well that the BDPI has not been able to nail him like they did to the other eight members of his gang some months back in Yakutia. If it is the last thing I do in this service, I will like to see that bastard Dima Kisa as he calls himself safely behind bars. He must be making his millions of dollars from selling cocaine and other hard drugs. But does he care to know how many lives he is destroying with the stuff he peddles so craftily all over the world?"

"My God, so the man is a cocaine dealer? No wonder he smells like so much money!"

"That is to tell you, my young colleague not all that glitters is gold. I am sure he went to that bank to deposit some of his ill gotten wealth or went to withdraw some of it. Dima Kisa may be smart, but at least I am one step near to landing him in jail."

Romanov looked curiously at his senior officer. "What do you mean by that sir?"

"There is something that drug dealers don't know and will never know." Pushkin said. "Although banks don't disclose the finances of their customers I have secretly got a directive from the cops highest boss to authorize the bank to let us know all manner of transactions that Dima Kisa makes. May be through that we may one day get him and throw him behind bars for life."

"I should say that is a smart move sir."

"Well, I don't know whether it is all that. But I hope it will help us to nail that drug baron." said detective Pushkin. He took out his cell phone and dialed a number which his younger colleague did not see as he spoke quietly. When he took the phone away from his ear, he said to his junior colleague. "Would you believe it Romanov, the bastard just went in and saved six hundred and fifty thousand dollars! Now tell me what kind of business must he be doing to get all that money?"

Romanov shook his head in perplexity. "If we know him to be a crook then why don't we just haul him out to jail?"

"On what charge Romanov? On what charge I ask? Don't you know we are a developed nation with the best democratic government and until you can prove that the man is guilty, you can't touch him? And God knows the drug man Dima Kisa has enough money to sue the entire cops if he is wrongly arrested. That is why the cop boss has asked us who are on his trail to be extra careful before nailing him."

"I see," Romanov said looking respectfully at his senior officer. "What do we do now sir?"

"We will drive back to the headquarters and I will brief you as my new assistant on how far we have collected some loose evidence on the man. Maybe with you joining the cops at Moscow from Yakutia where you were recently stationed, you may have some tricks up to help us catch that criminal."

The fact was corporal Romanov had only worked for a month since he was transferred to the BDPI headquarters from Yakutia where he had been known to do some very good work for the detective cops. Upon his arrival in Moscow, he was seconded to Pushkin to try and trap the drug baron Valadia Oleg also known as Dima Kisa. That explained the presence of the two of them at the bank in the unmarked cop car this morning.

Pushkin started the BDPI car and was about to drive away when he saw another person who had also just emerged out of the bank, he whistled low and sucked in his breath as he stared into the side mirror.

This time the person who emerged was a young beautiful woman in her late twenties. This one also looked like money was dripping out of every breath she exhaled. She wore a short red skirt and a casual sleeveless yellow blouse that was opened generously at the neck to show a sizeable portion of her beautiful breasts and was equally exposed. Her hair flowed beautifully behind her. Her big eyes set in so young and her face was fresh that made her very desirable indeed as a woman.

On her middle finger she swung a set of car keys.

As the cops watched her from the side mirror of their car, she walked purposefully with long and easy strides to a bright red Jaguar car that was as outstanding as she herself.

Sliding smoothly behind the seat of her car, she drove away in a burst of screeching tires.

As her car disappeared, Romanov turned to look at his senior officer again. Pushkin did not wait for him to ask a question, but said "Well, if you want to know who is that girl I will tell you. Everybody in Moscow calls her Lady Masha Alexy. But that is not the name her father gave her on her birthday. She was born Masha Alexy Nketia, but people only call her Lady Masha Alexy. And if you think she has any of the sterling qualities of those who bears the name Masha, then you are mistaken. For all I know she is one hell of a crook too. A crook that may well be in the category if not higher of that nasty Dima Kisa."

"And what kind of criminal activity does she also engage in to appear so rich sir?"

"That is the mystery. She claims to be an international hairdresser! Can you beat that? An international hairdresser! She has money coming to her from mysterious sources from overseas. But I have a feeling she is also tied to this drug business. What I am not sure of is whether she is working with that Dima Kisa who just left in that Benz. I would not be surprised if the two of them are linked somehow in this drug business."

Corporal Romanov shook his head in perplexity. "This Moscow is full of shady characters both men and women if I may say so sir."

"You can say that again. The unfortunate thing is that all of them are respected by this money crazy society as if they are saints. If I had my way all of them should be rotting in jail, but of course I can't do that. But this Lady Masha Alexy or whatever she calls herself is also of interest to the BDPI. And I will very much like to see her brought to book too."

Pushkin heaved a sigh and pulled the car out of the bank parking lot, drove forwards a bit and turned left towards of the Kwame Nkrumah street. He then angled his car out of the street and moved towards the Meklohemaklaya street.

He was on his way to report the results of his surveillance to his bosses at the cop headquarters. At last night came, Valodia Ivan lay beside Lena his wife hoping to doze off into an elusive sleep.

His mind was busy sorting out some issues that bothered him as his eyes darted vacantly at the blurry ceiling. The events of many meetings with Dima Kisa many months ago were very prominent to his mind.

"What am I going to do with this huge amount of money? Maybe it's time to join the league of fat account owners in some reputed banks in Europe and America." he mused to himself. He thought of going into estate development or acquire a number of houses in Russia and the oil rich nations of the world... no... The Russian cops would definitely be on my trail, but I can easily manipulate things at my favor." he soliloquized. He later dismissed such thoughts and resolved that the money would serve some important purposes at the right time.

At most in his mind was to try and avoid public notice. He was afraid of the press. They could really be troublesome and prying into other peoples business. One thing was certain if they hoped to continue to benefit from the drug business proceeds they must all use their official position to play ball exactly the way Dima Kisa wanted it.

The night was calm with good weather.

Valodia Ivan heaved a sigh after a long thinking. "It is going to be risky, rough and very tasking now that the cops have started suspecting Dima Kisa," he thought. In next to no time Dima Kisa's words began to intervene in his mind. "Crude oil is the diamond and girls mean money, real money." Those words hit him hard. He loved Lena his wife. He will not want her to know his support to the drug deals. However, what if Lena knew...? No! No! This question must not be completed. He thought and covered himself with a blanket and eventually slept.

5
_____

SOME weeks later, Dima Kisa left for the Champion club. It was a calm club for matured minded people. The breeze was gentle that Saturday evening. It was filled with some pleasant aroma that no doubt was produced by many beautiful flowers that adorned its environment. It was an ideal place for those in search of a place to hide from the rough and tumble of the city. The club offered great comfort and relaxation to tourists. This Saturday was an all young adults and adult night at the club.

The Champion club was a popular night spot in Moscow. Lady Masha Alexy, as she was now known in Moscow and beyond sat all alone at an exclusive table set on a platform. Under the soft blueish light of the Champion club, Masha Alexy's beauty really blossomed. The Champion club is much patronized by the young and rich people in Moscow. It is always full on the weekends.

It does not take any keen mind to know that Masha Alexy had what it takes to get the world moving. That is money. And even those who had never met her before and had also never heard of her knew the moment they saw her that this was not a lady to be trifled with. Not unless you had billions of money to spend yourself.

Men came near and slowly passed her table being very much aware that hers was not a table to be shared. The word EXCLUSIVE on a plaque had been placed on her table and there was no seat opposite to hers to invite anyone else to sit down with her.

From her vantage point, Masha Alexy could see the whole dancing floor, the bar and see the live band playing as well. The band was playing some soft blues that opened the night up to the young romantic couples who had come to enjoy themselves. The atmosphere in there at the Champion club was full of fun, just perfect for a relaxing evening and it was clear that all the people who had come there this Saturday night were looking for relaxation.

They had all toiled and labored throughout the week and today Saturday was the day to unwind and feel good.

Young and eager men circled the lady on the high table like predators, but backed away quickly enough when they saw the EXCLUSIVE sign that was placed on her table. If that did not define the prospective adventurer at all then the fact that on her table was a bottle of some very expensive vodka, champagne and a rich array of food.

Any man who showed any interest in her was quickly discouraged by the fact that if he was asked to pay for what was on her table it would take a whole month's pay to do that.

Self respecting and observant men might back away quickly from Masha Alexy's table the moment they saw it, but not all people at the Champion club that evening were self respecting or observant.

Before long a short brash man who had evidently been drinking too much approached the table of the young woman and greeted her in a voice loud enough to disturb a corpse.

Masha Alexy kept on looking at the live band on the stage as if nobody at all had spoken to her.

The man reeking of cheap alcohol bent near to her and almost screamed into her ear, "I said good evening young lady. My name is Zhena."

Masha Alexy Nketia raised her head and looked at the man for the first time. "Your name is Zhena so what? Look if it means anything to you I haven't asked to see anybody who bears the name Zhena."

Although the young drunk man smarted at this sharp rebuff from the woman he plodded bravely on. "It will not be a bad idea to know you baby."

Masha Alexy chuckled without any trace of humor. "Who is your baby?"

"You of course and I say it would not be a bad idea to get to know you better."

"Why?" Masha Alexy asked with a noticeable sneer.

"Well to begin with I Zhena can see that you are a beautiful lady and you are sitting alone. I was thinking perhaps you will need some company."

Masha Alexy shook her head in the manner of a woman who was experiencing an acute exasperation and said, "Zhena or whatever you call yourself I should have thought that you have eyes enough to know your kind of woman. I am not your kind of woman. Besides if I needed company and you were the only one around I would rather invite some self respecting cockroach to dine with me."

The insult stung Zhena so much that he moved back briefly to study the beautifully arrogant face of the young woman who had just spoken. He was about to say something nasty himself when at a secret signal from Masha Alexy. Two heavy muscled bodyguards emerged out of nowhere and bundled the man straight outside the Champion club.

Zhena was never seen again inside the Champion club that day.

Those men who had seen the treatment recently took out to the adventurism of Zhena and stayed as far away as possible from the table of Masha Alexy. They didn't want to be humiliated the way Zhena had.

Twenty minutes later, the band was still playing and Masha Alexy was quietly dining and drinking her champagne and enjoying the night. People had seen how she got Zhena quickly dispatched and those who had similar thoughts of trying to chart her up rapidly abandoned that idea.

But not everybody at the Champion club that night appeared to be scared of Masha Alexy Nketia. Not every man at the Champion club that day was so timid as to stay clear away from Masha Alexy. There was a man a few meters away who believed he had the right to every woman he wanted.

A few meters from her own EXCLUSIVE table was another EXCLUSIVE table occupied by a grey haired man who also sat quietly watching the live band. This man had a thick cigar stuck in one corner of his lips and he was puffing the smoke lazily into the night. On his table were some expensive drinks, but unlike Lady Masha Alexy he was not sitting alone. Opposite to him was a slim beauty of about twenty five who could have been his daughter.

But those who knew Dima Kisa would know that the young girl was neither his daughter nor a relative of any sort. The woman would be one of the girls the drug dealer called his play thing.

The fact was whenever Dima Kisa felt like chosing any girl or woman to spend the night with. And as soon as his sexual drive was satisfied he paid that female in question heavily off and then sent her out of his life forever. It was rumored that at fifty five years of age he had children littered all over the city with all kinds of women young and old. But in his palatial residence on the Dobreninskaya street he lived alone with his servants and bodyguards.

Any woman that came to his mansion was only brought there to entertain the boss and then to be paid off as soon as the boss felt entertained enough. The sad thing was because of the need for money women flocked to him at the snap of his fingers just to enjoy a portion of Dima Kisa's billions.

That he was a drug baron was no secret. But the fact that the cops had not been able to charge and convict him was what posed a mystery to most people. That also added to his fame as an untouchable. People even peddled the story around that he had cops who always informed him in advance of the movements of the cops on his activities.

Although the cops had conducted some hectic in house investigations to make sure that Dima Kisa had no cops he uses to access the cops activities, people still did not believe that he could act that way without the help of some law enforcement agent member. No person without cop protection could act with that impunity in Russia.

From where Masha Alexy Nketia sat at the bar she could not see the special seat of Dima Kisa. But the grey haired man with the cigar could see her and it did not take long for his interest to be aroused. Especially after the way she had Zhena disposed of.

Still puffing lazily at his cigar Dima Kisa scribbled a short note on a piece of paper and signaled his bodyguard who was standing at attention behind him to bend his head to his lips. Dima kisa then thrust the paper into the hands of the bodyguard who nodded and started walking away at the direction of Masha Alexy Nketia.

As soon as the bodyguard had gone Dima kisa looked at the young girl who sat opposite to him eating as if she was sure she would never get to eat a rich meal again.

"Natasha?" he called.

"Yes, what is it Dima?"

Dima Kisa pulled his cigar out of his mouth and looked levelly at the girl. "In a few minutes I will join by a woman I want to discuss business with. As soon as she comes I want you to excuse us for a few minutes. You can pretend you are going to the washroom then take a taxi home. I will arrange for my driver to bring two hundred dollars tomorrow to you."

The girl he was sitting with looked up at him. Her face was suddenly pale with pain. "Are you sending me away ignominiously because of another woman Dima Kisa?"

"I said I want to discuss a business proposition with her. And if you come up with any challenges again I will reduce the two hundred dollars I intend to give you by half. Any further protests it will be down again by half till you have nothing at all. And mind you if I want you taken away by force I have the men to do that. So behave and do just what I have told you Natasha."

The girl looked as if water had been poured on her when Dima Kisa spoke this way.

Slowly she stood up. "If that is what you want then I think it will be better for me to leave now Dima."

"No Natasha. You sit down untill that girl comes. As you may have heard about me I don't like being left alone in public places until I say so. Especially if I am paying the bills. So you will wait untill she comes then you get up and go."

The humiliation was too much for Natasha, but she appeared to be powerless against the drug man.

As if she was being controlled by a force she could not resist. Natasha sat down again. Indeed if it had not been money talking there was every indication that she would never stand for such humiliating treatment from the drug baron.

***

Masha Alexy Nketia was sitting quietly enjoying herself when the heavy muscled man placed the paper on her table and stood a few paces back and said, "the famous Dima Kisa asked me to bring you this letter. He is sitting a few tables behind you." said the man not knowing that Dima Kisa was watching them with the tail of his eyes.

If the bodyguard had expected Masha Alexy to jump and show all nervous at the name Dima Kisa, then he was sadly mistaken. The young Masha Alexy looked up and down at the bodyguard and asked, "who is this so called Dima Kisa?"

Masha Alexy's cold tone took the bodyguard back a bit.

"I am surprised you don't know my boss lady because everybody in Moscow here does. He is the famous international oil business man who sometime ago offered to give financial support to all the disabled people institutions of learning."

"Oh I see," Masha Alexy remarked casually. "Now I remember. Is he not the one who was announced as a crook by the government and roundly disgraced by the mass media?"

"That was the work of the detractors of my boss who didn't want him to help the common man lady."

"Well that is your version of the story. I didn't hear it that way. Anyway what is on this note that you have brought to me?"

"I wouldn't know lady. I am not expected to know what is in it."

"Never mind, you open it."

"With all due respects to you lady. It is your letter and I am not supposed to read it."

Masha Alexy appeared to be enjoying herself immensely at the expense of the ruffled bodyguard. "I am asking you to open it and I will read it. If not I will ask you to take it back to whoever gave it to you."

The bodyguard looked left and right in utter confusion and then back to where his boss sat. He then turned to look at Masha Alexy again.

"I said open it." Masha Alexy urged him. "I am authorizing you to open it."

Looking away from the letter the bodyguard opened the letter and straightened it on her table. Masha Alexy read the contents with a mischievous smile playing her lips.

Lady Masha Alexy

I have heard so much about you in business circles. And I have longed for the day I would see you face to face. I am sitting only a few tables at this EXCLUSIVE section behind you.

I will like you to join me at my table to discuss a few things of mutual interest. I am sending away the girl with me so we can have some privacy.

Dima Kisa

"Okay fold it up," Masha Alexy again ordered the bodyguard.

"What did you say lady?"

It was evident that the bodyguard was becoming angry at the antics of Masha Alexy, but he dared not show that anger especially as this was the new woman his boss was interested in.

"I said fold the letter up and take it back to your boss."

The bodyguard did that, but did not go away directly. "Should I tell him you are coming?"

"No don't tell him anything."

"Are you coming then?"

Masha Alexy introduced a tinge of anger into her voice. "Will you do just as I say or I will report you to your so called boss?"

At this sharp retort the bodyguard quickly took the paper and walked back to his boss. Taking secret looks behind her, Masha Alexy could see Dima Kisa heatedly interrogating his bodyguard. She smiled. It was not that she had never heard of Dima Kisa or Valadia Oleg as it was his real name. Nobody in Moscow could say he or she had not heard of that drug baron. But being a woman of means herself Masha Alexy had no wish to be made a play thing of that morally a corrupt drug baron. That was why she had deliberately made the man appear as he was nobody to her.

Then again out of the corner of her eyes she saw the elderly drug baron himself attempting to get up from his seat. Masha Alexy quickly got up first from her own seat and saw the smile of contentment on Dima Kisa's face as he sat back down. In his mind that single lady at the exclusive table had at last decided to join him.

He watched Masha Alexy closely as she took her hand bag from the back rest of her chair and left a generous tip for the waiter who had come to serve her. She then hung the bag across her shoulders and started walking towards the table of Dima Kisa.

Masha Alexy was amused to see the cheap girl who was sitting with the drug baron who quickly got up and left. What a shame that some species a woman kind allowed themselves to be used cheap. Masha Alexy Nketia would never allow herself to be treated this way by any man she vowed.

Just when she was about a meter from the table of the big man, Masha Alexy turned towards the main door of the Champion club and walked smartly out. A few minutes after she drove away in her red sports jaguar.

Nobody in the Champion club that night failed to see how the young so called international hairdresser Masha Alexy snubbed the fabulously rich drug dealer Dima Kisa.

That was the day Dima Kisa swore that he would get Masha Alexy in his bed or try dying. He would use her and humiliate her the way she had humiliated him in public. Dima Kisa, whom the cops fear to touch to be made so small by this girl Masha Alexy whom he could father was a shock. Nobody dared to treat Dima Kisa this way in Moscow and live to boast about it. And like hell Masha Alexy wouldn't be the first.

He would get her.

He would exact his revenge and it will be a thousand times more than the way she had humiliated him.

6

IT was on a Friday just at 7:40 pm. A convoy of three black cars sneaked into the car parking lot of the club 13 through the entrance gate of the compound. The right back door was opened by one of the security men of the club. Dima Kisa climbed down. He put his right hand into the pocket of his suit and brought out a wrap of two hundred dollars cash and threw it at the security man who hurriedly grabbed them in the air as if they would disappear if they touched the ground.

"Thank you sir, thank you sir," he said repeatedly. He behaved like one who was seeing money for the first time in his life. Perhaps he had not seen that amount of money all at once before.

Dima Kisa did not respond to his greetings as he screwed up his stern looking face and walked to the reception. The man watched him wondering what kind of man his benefactor was as he surveyed him with the aid of the electric bulbs that illuminated the compound. This was his sixteenth year at the gate of the club yard and had never had it so good like that day. Some customers who visited the club at times gave out trips to staff, but none had ever received anything above one euro.

"What a man he was… very generous… may this man never lack… may God never fail to protect and guide him as he remembers the poor every day of his life… may this club never lack such generous customers… may those customers who find it very difficult to help poor people never find their way to this club again. May the pockets that produced this money expand its hand of generosity to people everywhere it goes…" the security man continued to say his prayers not minding that the man had gone out of sight. Occupants of the cars merely watched him and laughed in disbelief.

"Poverty is dangerous. It could make a man and woman do unimaginable things… lick the wounds of a rich man." the driver said.

"Does it end there alone? The person will lick a rich man's shoes… anus… his urine and faeces all because of money." whispered another occupant of the car who found the security man's behavior very disgusting.

Suddenly, the security man took it to his heels. He hid himself among the flowers. He continued to force and squeeze himself into the flowers. He had seen a man emerge from the reception and took it to his heels. The security man thought the man was Dima Kisa, who may have changed his mind and was coming to take his money back. His whole eyes turned wildly red.

"Never, I said never! Unless I am killed before I will allow this to happen. Yes, I will not live to see it happen," he murmured as he ran away.

Some rich men were like that. Whenever they gave out something they must have carefully planned how to get it back even if it means reaping many times more then what they gave out. It was just like giving with one hand and drawing it back with the other. This was their attitude and men knew, but had no better option than to be used by these men.

The following day was Saturday, Dima Kisa was relaxing on the roof of his palatial house on the Dobreninskaya street with a different girl this time.

This was a young one too. He was sipping the Russian vodka lazily from a tall glass when the cell phone rang. He was laying on his back and relaxing on a soft mat. The girl with him, wore a skimpy swim suit. As soon as Dima Kisa heard who was calling, he asked the girl to go downstairs to the swimming pool and give him a little privacy.

As soon as the girl left, Dima Kisa spoke softly into the phone, "Kolia is that you?"

"Yes boss. It is Kolia speaking," the voice said at the other end.

"I am listening Kolia," Dima Kisa said in his heavy voice. "Is everything ok?"

"Boss, you have to check your steps well."

"I have always been doing that. Have you heard anything new?"

"I am speaking from Siberia now. It looks like the cops are hot on their heels for your finances. I have made some investigations at the bank. It is as if somebody there has been giving the cops details of your monetary transactions with them. They even know you went and deposited six hundred and fifty thousand United States dollars two weeks ago."

If the information shook the drug baron, it did not show on his face. "I see does the bank manager know this, K?"

"No boss, I have checked. The manager is clean. But I am sure there is a cop plant in the bank who is supplying the cops with information of your business dealings."

"I heard you. It looks like this Pushkin and his gangs are getting bolder. Thanks for the information, K. If the cops think they are smart they don't know that I also have my own secret sources among them. This information you have given me is worth two thousand dollars. You can collect it at the usual place tomorrow. If you can find out who exactly the cop planted at my bank I promise you an extra two thousand Kolia."

"Yes sir. Thank you very much. I will be at the usual point to collect it boss."

The conversation ended and just as the mysterious Kolia who was obviously one of Dima Kisa's bodyguards doubled as a secret agent rang off and his cell phone rang again. Dima kisa took the phone quickly to his ear again thinking it was the mysterious Kolia who had forgotten to tell him something. "Is that you again, Kolia?"

A feminine voice spoke quickly into the phone. "No it is not Kolia. It is me!"

Dima Kisa was instantly animated. Women always had that effect on him. "You? Excuse me lady, but I don't think I have ever had the pleasure of hearing your sweet voice anywhere," Dima Kisa spoke in his best seductive voice having visions of another female prey to add to his growing list of conquest.

"We have met before, but I am afraid to say at that time it was not under any circumstances.

Well my name is Masha Alexy Nketia. People in Moscow call me Lady Masha Alexy."

Dima Kisa sucked in his breath remembering that night of humiliation at the hands of this girl at the Champion club. "Oh my God, it's you."

"Yes it's me, are you surprised?"

"How did you get my phone number?"

"That is not necessary now. What is necessary is that I am approaching your house now in my car so get your bodyguard preferably the one you asked to bring me the letter at the Champion club to open it for me. I have to see you."

"Why do you have to see me Masha Alexy?" he was not going to add the lady to make this girl feel important.

"Of course I should not have bothered you and I don't even know why I am doing this, but Dima Kisa, I have information that is crucial to your survival."

"I don't think I get the drift of what you are saying," Dima Kisa said, suddenly feeling his muscles stiffen with anxiety. "How could you possibly have information that is crucial to my survival? I don't think I am in any noticeable danger. Not I Dima Kisa."

"If that is what you think then I believe I am just wasting my time. Sorry for bothering you.

Forget I called. I will just turn my car around and go back where I came from."

Dima Kisa did not know whether this girl was just bluffing, but the way she had sounded so sure of herself she might truly have some information that might benefit him. Hadn't it been rumored after all that she is also in the drug business? It might be useful to hear what this Lady Masha Alexy had to say to him. "Hang on Masha Alexy. I am not simply dismissing you. But I would like to have a hint of what you have to tell me."

"On the phone?"

"Why not, Masha Alexy?"

Masha Alexy laughed at the other end. "Well what about this? I have information of a cop plant at your bank who is giving them details of all your financial transactions."

The expression on Dima Kisa's face could not be totally described as shock, but there was a great deal of anxiety there. "In that case I will see you. How soon do you think you can get to my place here?"

"I am near the mighty Volgino club building. Let's say I will be at your place in three minutes."

"Don't drive too fast to kill yourself. I will like to hear what you have to say."

"Don't worry about me Dima Kisa. I have been driving since the age of twelve. I can handle cars. And you don't smoke those nasty cigars to cut short a beautiful life of crime before the devil takes his own."

"In so many ways I am like you Masha Alexy. We are both the children of the devil."

"You are the first born Dima Kisa you must be more menacing."

Dima Kisa laughed loudly at the other end. "If there is one human being I have waited so long to meet personally in this world it is you. So do come quickly."

Before Masha Alexy switched off her phone Dima Kisa was

screaming for his bodyguard to go and open the door for the red jaguar that would be coming to see him in a few minutes.

But something puzzled him. His own man Kolia had just rung him to tell him of the cop planted at the bank. And then just a few seconds after this Lady Masha Alexy whom he had heard was also in the drug business had rung to warn him of the same plant. How had she come by that information? More importantly how had she come by his personal cell phone number?

Were his business activities transparent that all people knew what he was doing and how to get in touch with him at anytime?

He had to know so much about this Lady Masha Alexy. In addition to having this Masha Alexy in his bed Dima Kisa thought she would also be an interesting ally.

7

THE moment Lady Masha Alexy was ushered into the living room of Dima Kisa's house the famed peddler began to literally lick his lips in anticipation of a hearty female meal.

He was like a snake which had just bite a relaxing lizard. He licked his lips and rubbed his crotch in a wickedly obscene manner. No person looking at him could fail to see what dirty thoughts were circling in his mind. Masha Alexy certainly knew what he was thinking. And she was going to have none of it, at least not this day.

The provocative manner in which Lady Masha Alexy was herself dressed invited those sexual thoughts and overt sexual actions from Dima Kisa. She was in a short indeed very short jeans skirt and the blouse she had on top just stopped short of covering her navel. The high heels on which she stood somehow managed to emphasize her ample buttocks and on her lips was a cheeky red lipstick that warned all and sun dry that this was a worldly wise girl who should not be toyed with.

Dima Kisa was dressed up in a pair of khaki shorts and a

loose blue t shirt, but he never stopped rubbing his crotch from time to time to indicate his lecherous intentions.

As soon as Masha Alexy made her sexy entrance she did not allow the owner of the house to offer her a seat, but went and threw herself on the long couch and crossed one leg dangerously over the other. As she crossed and uncrossed her legs she was aware that her silky white panties showed themselves from time to time. But that was what she intended. Indeed the way she was seated and the way she was dressed she left very little of what was under the clothes to the imagination.

"I don't know what to say whether to say I am thrilled to have you here or surprised considering that the last time I invited you to join me at the Champion club you ran away from me."

Masha Alexy kept studying the fish that was swimming in the beautiful aquarium placed on the table against the wall. "The last time you invited me to join you at the Champion club I did not run away from you. I had other things to do on that day and you were not in my agenda."

Very few people would dare to talk to the famous Dima Kisa this way especially very few women. This Masha Alexy had to have something special to be this bold.

Dima Kisa gulped at this woman's plucky attitude. "For a woman you sound very cocky and brave considering that you snubbed me before, but have yourself invited yourself into my den so to speak."

Lady Masha Alexy tossed her bounteous hair seductively behind her and brushed the loose hair over her face back onto her head. "When I invited myself into your house I had the thought that I was going to discuss something with you that would save your neck. Because of that I did not think you would have any harmful thoughts towards me. But if you think because I am in your house you can attack me in any way you are invited to try."

The veiled venom in the woman's voice did not escape the famed drug baron. "Is that a threat I detect in your voice?"

"You don't know me so you can decide on how I sound,"

Masha Alexy replied evasively.

"You sound very clever Masha Alexy, but I don't want you to forget that as Dima Kisa I have a reputation of this city of Moscow."

"A reputation as what? Rapist? A torturer? Or a murderer?"

"I am not saying that, but…"

"Look Dima Kisa if you intend to rape, torture or kill me because I have come to your house that would not in the least bit frighten me. Do I look like a woman who is afraid of rape or torture or death? Indeed if you are to rape me which I think is your intention that would lower my estimation of you."

"How do you estimate me?" Dima Kisa asked uncertainly. For the first time in his life he was unsure of himself in front of a woman.

"I have heard of your reputation as a good chaser of women. I have heard that you have the capacity to sweet talk them into bed. I have never heard people say you force them to sleep with you. In addition to saving your neck I came here to give you the opportunity I denied you that night at the Champion club."

"What opportunity did you deny me?" Dima Kisa asked suspiciously.

"I came here Dima Kisa to give you the opportunity to talk me into your bed. But I should say I am sad by the crude manner you have started this business with veiled threats of wanting to rape me. If that is what you want to do go ahead. I won't resist you and see if you can enjoy me."

Throughout Dima Kisa's life, he had never met any woman who stood up to him in such a base way as this Masha Alexy did. He had heard that her tag as an international hairdresser was just a front. It was rumored that she was also in the drug peddling business. If it was true then that explained her tough stance against the most fearsome, but urban crook in the Moscow metropolis.

Dima Kisa decided to change tacks to see if he could catch Masha Alexy on the wrong foot.

"You intrigue me, err… lady err…"

"Masha Alexy," she supplied. "I am surprised you have forgotten my name already, seeing I have not forgotten yours. Or is it one of your courting tricks?"

She was a smart talker surely, but Dima Kisa was determined to put her under his big foot. He shook his head to clear it and avoided answering her question. "That's right, Masha Alexy. You interest me. Is your business as an international hairdresser exactly what you do?"

"Oh no, not only that," Masha Alexy said sarcastically, "I double up as a bicycle repairer too."

She then looked straight into Dima Kisa's face. "I should say coming from the famous Dima Kisa that is a pretty dumb question you have asked me. Suppose I had asked you if the oil business you claim you are doing is the only one thing you do, will you answer me?"

Dima Kisa stood still nodding at the cleverness of this young girl. "I will grant you that I would not tell you if I had another secret job going for me. So I made a mistake asking you about your real profession. Okay let's forget that. Now my next question, how did you get my phone number?"

"Any person I develop interest in, in this city, I can get that person's phone number. So let's drop that question too. Now I will ask my own questions. Did you or did you not go to deposit six hundred and fifty thousand dollars last week?"

Dima Kisa looked steadily at the young woman. "I will prefer not to answer that question. But why do you ask Masha Alexy?"

"It is because a cop plant at the bank is feeding the cops every detail of transactions you make at the bank. And they are not doing this because they have your welfare at heart. Dima Kisa the cops are doing this because they want to throw you to jail and keep you there forever."

"I see why would they want to throw an honest business man like me to jail?" Dima Kisa asked.

At this question Masha Alexy bent over and laughed out loud. When she could control herself a little, she looked at Dima Kisa's face and almost vibrating with a suppressed laughter and said. "Honest business man indeed! Tell me another fairy tale Dima Kisa."

"Well let's try this other fairy tale then," Dima Kisa paced his hall a bit and then turned suddenly and asked. "I even forgot to offer you a drink. What will you take?"

"Now you are remembering to be a gentleman. I thought you would never ask. Gin and lime will do for me if you have it and don't spike it with any sleeping tablets. I am too smart for that."

"With you I wouldn't even dream of giving cabin biscuits," he laughed and Masha Alexy did too. "Now I will be interested to know how you came by that information."

"I will also prefer to keep that as part of my intelligent secret. I wanted to be helpful by volunteering this information. If I have been helpful in anyway, then I would like to be excused. I have other things to attend to."

"No lady, you are not going until you tell me a few things I want to know. I say who gave you that information?"

Masha Alexy sat there for some minutes swinging her legs like someone who could no longer tolerate a situation. "Okay if this would interest you, I have my own secret sources from the cops. I pay them and they give me information as to what the incorruptible cop men are planning to do. They give me the information and I always stay one step ahead of the cops. My paid informers in the cop force were giving me personal information to me when you were mentioned. I could have kept that information and let them nail you. But as a nice sister in business I decided to hint you. Have I done wrong?"

Dima Kisa stood there nodding his grey head. "No you have done very right. Indeed you have as much as admitted that you are not an honest business person like myself."

"When did I say that?" Masha Alexy queried.

"Any sweet looking woman like you who pays the cops to give her information on the honest cop men can't be honest herself. So we are both in the same nasty boat aren't we Masha Alexy?"

"I refuse to answer that question."

Dima Kisa laughed out loud. "I would thank you for the information you brought, but I should also say that was totally unnecessary."

"Oh, so you mean I wasted my time coming to talk to you?"

"No Masha Alexy I didn't say that. But I am only saying that your information, though accurate came a bit too late. I have also got my own men in the force, who promptly inform me if things are threatening to go against me. You did not think somebody like me would take precautions, would you? I was given the information you have just given me just two days ago," Dima lied smoothly.

"In that case sorry to have wasted your time I will like to be excused."

"Not so fast lady. There are other things you and I will have to talk about now that you are here things that will ensure our mutual survival in our common businesses. Now if you will tell me the kind of job you really do I will introduce you to my informer. He is very high up in cop hierarchy and I bet he will be more useful and up to date than your paid informers in the force. Are you also in the white powder business if I may be bold to ask? And please come clean with me."

Masha Alexy sat there for a long time looking into the face of the drug baron and finally admitted. "You know that is what I do. But what the hell, I don't like advertising the fact."

Dima Kisa was laughing now. "Neither do I. But it is important that we in the brotherhood or should I say sisterhood know each other so that we don't cross paths and also for us to share information that will benefit one another. Why do I say this? You will agree with me that if one of us is thrown into prison it will make the others still in the business very vulnerable don't you think?"

Masha Alexy sat there for a long time as if finding it difficult to make up her mind. "Dima Kisa you are right." she said.

"Good now that we both know where we stand, will you be my guest at a small party I am throwing tomorrow evening? I will introduce you to my man in the cop force and I assure you it will be profitable to know him. Incidentally his name is Kolia."

Without waiting to hear if Masha Alexy would stay or not, Dima Kisa took his cell phone and dialed Kolia's number.

He spoke quickly into the phone. "Kolia I will like you to join me at a small party I am throwing tomorrow evening for only three people. I want you to meet one lady of distinct in Moscow too."

The next day Dima Kisa was in his office working when Valodia Ivan walked into his office with noisy steps that appeared intended to crush the hard concrete floor. He looked angry. He never cared to sit down even when Dima Kisa asked him to do so.

"What has happened to my share of money from your last deal?" he asked with a fixed stare at Dima Kisa.

"You have no share in my deals any more…"

"Why?" Valodia Ivan replied.

"You have not been using your office well to protect the business and so you have no share again," Dima Kisa explained.

"Then I will expose your dirty deal…"

"Is it my dirty deals alone?"

"Yes! It's all yours and I will expose you."

"Fool! Fool! Look at yourself, a rat that I gave hope when he was hopeless. Today, you have lost your respect and manners to the extent that you now walk into my office and point at me… now get out of my office."

Valodia Ivan laughed. "You are an idiot!"

"Thank you, but leave my office."

"I shall do that, but not until I get an explanation on what happened to my share of money from our recent deals."

Dima Kisa refused to talk.

"You deceived me to give you all my support. You told me that you would pay me twenty thousand dollars, but you lied, instead you eat my own shares. Dima Kisa I want an answer and I demand for it now," the visitor roared with rage hitting his hand severally on the table.

"Two things that break relationships are women and money,

believe it or leave it. No man ever became rich that kept his hands clean.

It is either you duped or cheated your fellow to make your

fortune or you killed so it's not evil if I had cheated you in any form you think of."

"So you are now biting the finger that has been feeding you Dima Kisa? Well I will forgive you because of our relationship if not I will make sure I use my position in the government to punish you," the man roared in anger.

Dima Kisa couldn't control his anger anymore. He stood up and rushed towards Valodia Ivan. He grabbed him and threw ceaseless punches at him until he fell and sprawling on the cold floor. He was now soaked in his own blood and beside him lay a tooth out of the many that was in his mouth. Dima Kisa ordered his boys to carry Valodia Ivan's corpse to the bush and bury him.

"Yes sir," the boys said. They had no other option than to carry out their boss's order. Valodia Ivan's body was carried outside to be buried. Dima Kisa was a strong man, no man that has received his punches when he gets angry ever to survive. He had fists of steel and had sent many to their untimely graves with his deadly blows. The boys took the corpse to a place where it could be identified by the owners and dumped Valodia Ivan's body. They had put themselves in the dead man's shoes and remembered that they had uncles were about the dead man's age.

8

DIMA KISA hanged up the telephone receiver and hurled himself back into the chair. He had just walked back home from his office. He looked happy and wore a glowing smile. "What an opportunity to make some quick money," he thought. He was silent for a while and gazed at the large party room in his house he had painstakingly decorated a few months back. Everything still looked perfect. He grabbed an electronic calculator, punched a few buttons and nodded satisfactorily. Just then, the door opened and Masha sauntered in. She was well mannered and beautiful, with a wonderful sense of clothing unlike yesterday when she visited Dima Kisa.

Dima Kisa fixed his eyes on her face until she sat nearby. He was fond of doing this because he thought the lady who just walked in could be made shy from his hard look on the face. Dima Kisa enjoyed this and often referred to it as eye lashing whenever he spoke to his friends about woman.

"I told you I will honor your invitation for the party and you doubted me." the lady said.

"Oh you are most welcome…"

"Where is your friend you equally called to join us?" the lady interrupted.

"He will soon be here," Dima Kisa replied. "You see I was working on some files in my office when I remembered that I had an appointment with you and my friend at my house this very evening so I quickly suspended all I was doing to be here all to show you how much I have appreciated and valued you."

"Alright, thank you for that." the lady said.

Dima Kisa laughed and adjusted his seat. He had not for once lifted off his eyes from the lady. His eyes were no doubt filled with lust. Right there in his mind he thought of different things all bordering on one issue. This same issue had remained on his mind ever since the lady failed to honor his invitation at the club. Then Dima Kisa initiated a business idea and they began to share ideas on how to make the business work for both of them. But Dima Kisa never meant all he was talking about. He only was creating a good opportunity to have much lustful look at the lady.

Soon there was silence.

"Why are you staring at me?"

Dima Kisa said nothing. What he had seen in the lady was a confirmation of his earlier appraisal. He had scored her above ninety five percent right from the first day he met her. This has been confirmed from what they were discussing. His friends and business partners had always warned him about lusting after women. But this time he saw his guest as a marriage material his possible future wife.

Again the door opened and Dima Kisa's friend walked into the party room. He was dressed in a cream Italian suit. For once he looked like a gentleman with a clean shaved face. He sat down and crossed both legs with an expectant look at Dima Kisa. Then Dima Kisa made the formal introduction of Kolia to his new catched lady as a cop and the lady to Kolia as a woman in the drug business. Kolia and Masha Alexy exchanged greetings and then the small party of three began.

Masha Alexy had left her seat and sat exactly opposite to Kolia as she ate the lobster that had been served with her meal.

If Kolia had heard of Masha Alexy or seen her anywhere before he did not show any sign of that. Indeed he seemed not to be too happy that Dima Kisa was introducing him as his helper in the cop force. But he later did not seem to mind as he got to know that all three of them sitting there were crooks. Indeed he even became animated when Masha Alexy asked him if the cops would have any of their honest agents at the airport the following Thursday.

"Why do you ask that?" Kolia asked.

"I hope to send five of my girls to Amsterdam. They will swallow the pellets of cocaine and later defecate them out when they reach Holland. I don't want them to be delayed unnecessarily," Masha Alexy said. "I have already taken care of the customs men and women at the Moscow Sheromentova International airport. Still I don't want to encounter any unforeseen opposition that is why I ask."

Kolia looked at her and said. "With all due respects to you Masha Alexy..."

"Call me Lady Masha Alexy."

"Lady Masha Alexy," the masked cop man Kolia laughed and said, "Don't you think you should be getting that kind of information from your own agent in the cop force?"

At this point Dima Kisa laughed out loud and announced, "Masha Alexy what Kolia wants to tell you is that he doesn't give valued information out freely. If you seek beneficial information from him you know what to do."

"Oh I see," so saying Masha Alexy brought out her handbag and pulled out a thick load of fifty dollars cash, peeled off ten of them and handed them to Kolia, with easy abandon. "This is money for the information I need Kolia. If you can get it for me before Thursday that would award you additional money."

Kolia's eyes nearly popped out of their sockets at the amount of money he was given. Masha Alexy was the type of people he liked to deal with. The crooked money men and women in the society.

He helped them and they helped him. If it weren't for people like Dima Kisa and Lady Masha Alexy, how could he build the mighty house he had built for himself at the country side and run a transport business in his wife's name? How much at all did he earn as a cop officer?

Kolia sat up straight. "Well by this time tomorrow, I will get you the information you need through Dima Kisa. If there will be any of the honest cops there at all I will show you where they will be stationed at the airport. Those like myself who will be there, don't worry about them. I will give them some of the money you have given me so that they will look the other way when your girls are passing through customs on their way to Amsterdam."

Masha Alexy shook Kolia's hand to seal the deal and future friendship. "Now if I may ask a stupid question is your real name Kolia?"

Both men at the table laughed out loud and Masha Alexy joined them too.

Eventually Kolia answered the question. "I am glad you yourself say it is a stupid question. So I will answer it stupidly. Yes, my real name is Kolia. My other names are Andrei and Sergei Louda."

The friendly laughter that exploded lasted for more than two minutes before Kolia asked to take his leave. Dima Kisa came back and met Masha Alexy still waiting for him in the party room.

He staggered in and slumped onto his seat filled with joy.

Not long Masha Alexy went into a long kissing session with Dima Kisa, but would not allow the old man to have his way down there. She made him to believe that she was in her menstral period and would oblige him in two days time when she was free. Dima Kisa was so excited he could barely contain himself. However, he elicited a strong promise from her to sleep with him before she leaves with her girls to Holland on Thursday.

That was when Masha Alexy came up with the bright idea. She looked straight into Dima Kisa's face and asked, "Why don't you accompany me to Holland on Thursday so that we could have a really smashing night in Amsterdam after we disembark at the Schiphol airport." Dima Kisa smiled.

He quickly jumped at the idea. "Hey that will be really cool! Yes Amsterdam will be a good idea on Thursday. I know of some swank hotel where we could spend the night. It overlooks a beautiful canal. You know Holland is full of canals. And I might use the opportunity to do some business myself as soon as Kolia gives us the all clear signal to Leningrad on Thursday.

Masha Alexy thumped the old cocaine baron playfully in the nose and kissed him on the lips.

"You still call the St. Petersbourg International airport, Leningrad International Airport? Don't you know the government has changed the name?"

Dima Kisa held her and kissed her full on the lips. "Old habits die hard. I have always known that airport as Leningrad and it will take me a long time to get used to the new name. As Leningrad that airport has brought a lot of luck to me. I don't want to call it any other name for fear of catching bad luck."

"I understand" said the lady. "But please don't forget to take some Viagra along on Thursday," Masha Alexy said.

"You mean sex enhancing tablets?"

"Yes," Masha Alexy said. "Please get your bodyguard to drive my car to the door." she teased.

"The very one you made a fool of at the Champion club?"

"Yes!" Masha Alexy said again and stepped out of the doorway near of Dima Kisa.

"He would look forward to the trip from the Moscow International airport to Amsterdam on Thursday." Masha Alexy said in her mind with a smile then she left.

Four hours later Valodia Ivan's house wore a mournful look that same evening. Lena and her friends yelled and cursed in agony. Her children who could not bear the terror, threw themselves on the hard floor in search of solace. Men sat lonely and speechless and Dimitry Misha looked dejected. Many security officers in Valodia Ivan's house cast vacant gaze at the sky as if solutions to their problems lay behind the cloud. Faces were screwed up with their problems lay behind the cloud. Faces were screwed up with crease suggesting nothing, but shattered dreams. Among the cops around it was only Dimitry Misha that seemed ready to change the situation as they paced up and down the compound with their faces growling like wild cats. The search for the murderer began instantly.

9

THE following day Maxism Ivanova staggered into his living room after the office hour and threw himself onto a sofa. His countenance exhibited nothing, but rage. "Dima Kisa... I've been a fool. We worked together, drank together as if we were brothers... no! No! Dima Kisa you are neither a brother nor a friend. I never knew you, but now I know you better... Dima... you are evil... wicked and without an atom of human sympathy. You had the mind to kill Valodia Ivan and took the entire share that was due for him now you want to take my own share too... never!" he sighed and shook his head. At this point he broke down and wept with guilt though he made efforts to control himself. "If I had known I wouldn't have gone into this dirty business. I regret it all. If the government finds out that I am among those who had over the years giving coverage to Dima Kisa's evil drug business how would my friends and family feel? Certainly it's going to tear my dearly beloved family to shreds.... I never bargained for this at all," he sighed again and bowed his head in disgust.

Maxism Ivanova knew the whole details on how Valodia Ivan was killed from Dimitry Misha's investigation report. The truth is that Dima Kisa killed Valodia Ivan. But Maxism Ivanova's surprise is that Dimitry Misha did not see something wrong with Dima Kisa's act. He believed that what he did was a sign of his hard work to make money for himself.

That evening Maxism Ivanova invited Dima Kisa for a drink at his house. Initially Dima Kisa was surprised because both had never had anything to discuss and hardly spoke to each other except on official capacity. Each felt superior and preferred to remain in a world of his own. He wondered why Maxism Ivanova wanted to see him. He didn't want to honor the invitation for some personal reasons which centered on the security investigation of who killed Valodia Ivan. But after some vacillations he decided to honor the unexpected invitation.

Dima Kisa was surprised to meet Dimitry Misha when he walked into the house, but he pretended never to have any doubt that the meeting was for evil.

"So where are the drinks?" Dima Kisa asked.

Maxism Ivanova offered drinks to his business associates as they all sat down. In between the drink the discussion began.

"We've realized how unimportant we are to the success of your business these days and how you could build your future on it even if we do not team up," Dimitry Misha said.

"Why all this talk?" Dima Kisa asked.

"Our future is bleak in your hands so we have invited you here to tell you that we have decided to pull out, face our work and leave you to carry your deals alone… "

"What nonsense are you talking about?" Dima Kisa interrupted Maxism Ivanova. "You know what this business is all about… money… people… connection… and I will not get any of these without us working in partnership."

"You have all that. You built a new partner the day you stopped giving us our due shares from the business proceeds. So we have decided to let you be," Dimitry Misha said.

"No!... no... no! It's not true. Your informants are wrong. Your whole idea is unfair and hard to imagine..."

"Wait Dima Kisa, nobody here is a kid to be toyed with. In this business, I single handed gave you hope... Maxism Invanova brought you out of those dirty dark cells surrounded by mighty walls that discourage one from the thoughts of breaking away... I did it with Valodia Ivan, but today where are we in your business train? No Dima! We have declined and shall not be a part of your deals again."

"Thank you so much I heard you well," Dima Kisa said. He got up and wanted to go, but Dimitry Misha was faster and he blocked the exit door and held him back.

"Please sit down... please go back to your seat..." he waited patiently and watched Dima Kisa walk back to the seat.

"Dimitry Misha and Maxism Ivanova has actually done a lot for me, but then we can't remain together forever in this deal. I cannot continue to depend on them all my life to move my deals forward. I have gotten new partners whom I pay very little to do what they have been doing for me over the past years. Now that both of them have realized that they are not useful to me anymore, I think the best is to buy their idea and discard them like a waste pack into the bin who suffers it? Both of them, yet I will remain comfortable, happy and satisfied," Dima Kisa said in his thought.

"Well, there is a report that you are fully responsible for the death of Valodia Ivan," Dimitry Misha said.

Dima Kisa was shocked to his marrow.

"We do not want to hand you over to the security agents because we know we have all been partners in all your actions. But we have to think of our future and free ourselves from shackles," Dimitry Misha added.

"I am not a party to Valodia Ivan's death. But I wish you could create a chance for us to meet at my house for a talk on this issue so that both of us will know who has been our enemies over the years." Dima Kisa said.

"No your house is not safe for this talk Dima Kisa. You will have much advantage over us if we do not agree with you on any issue raised at the meeting..."

"Then where do you suggest we meet?" Dima Kisa interrupted Maxism Ivanova.

"Let us meet at my house," Dimitry Misha said.

"But we will not be free to discuss important issues at your house like we will at my house. Your children will all be around so how do you think it will be possible?"

"My family went on a holidays so I am all alone at the wide compound except for my guards. To avoid the presence of the guards. Our discussions will be done at my resting garden beside the swimming pool," Dimitry Misha explained.

"Oh that is a good place," replied Dima Kisa. "What is our meeting time?"

"On Tuesday by noon," Maxism Ivanova said.

Dima Kisa stood again and made for the exit door. This time nobody stopped him. They sat down watching him open the door and walked out of the house.

"Dimitry Misha in this situation what do we do?"

"That's why I called you for this meeting." Maxism Ivanova said. He held his glass of wine and remained silent for a while. He thought of something, but nothing seemed reliable now. "We have to do whatever we feel is the best, but bear in mind that we have only a day to set ourselves free from Dima Kisa's blackmail because of our decision. But we must be careful, very careful," he added.

Dimitry Misha apparently lost in thought.

"Now that Dima Kisa has seen that he cannot lure us into his dirty deals any more and that we are aware of him being responsible for the death of Valodia Ivan, he will single handedly mastermind our death using his hit men. To avoid this evil occurrence from coming through he must be killed if he ventures to be at the meeting tomorrow." said Maxism Ivanova.

"Then what happens if he does not come?"

"We will sort for other ways to lure him into trouble and get him killed before he will make us lose our job."

Dimitry Misha nodded.

Maxism Ivanova insisted and prepared to execute his plans. They resolved to search for a perfect means of killing Dima Kisa the next day. They felt there was no point allowing him to live once he attends the meeting tomorrow. After all Dimitry Misha and Maxism Ivanova were man enough to decide on what they wanted and they resolved never to allow anything disturb their plans.

The next day was Tuesday and an office hour. Superintendent Pushkin spoke to his assistant who was sitting opposite to his table at the office at the cop headquarters. "What have you got so far on Dima Kisa since we last saw him two weeks ago corporal Romanov?"

"I was even about to come to your office to give you this information I have gathered on him when you summoned me here, sir."

"That's good," Pushkin beamed. "You have been very fast on him. What have you got so far?"

"Lets say sir, I am about to kill two birds with one stone. Through my own secret contacts I have been able to establish that that Dima Kisa is working hand in gloves with the lady we saw at the bank too."

Pushkin sat upright in his chair suddenly very animated. "You mean Lady Masha Alexy?"

"Yes sir. I mean Lady Masha Alexy Nketia," corporal Romanov said proudly.

He looked at his boss for sometime and added "From my very reliable sources the two of them would be traveling to Amsterdam in Holland on Saturday next week. It is supposed to be a business trip, but between you and me sir we know what business the two of them engage in. I suggest we station our men there from Friday night. The pair are clever. I hear Lady Masha Alexy will be flying first on Saturday on a British Caledonian aircraft at 11p.m. and Dima Kisa will follow up twenty four hours later on Sunday on a KLM flight. They don't want to appear as if they are traveling together. If we accost Lady Masha Alexy first, we will search her and keep her arrest a secret until we trap Dima Kisa the following day too. If we don't do that and we allow the press to go to town on the arrest of Masha Alexy, Dima Kisa would promptly abandon his trip and quickly recoil into his shell and it would be very difficult to get him again thereafter."

"That is some fast one," the superintendent said. "If we nail this pair I will make sure you are promoted and rewarded handsomely, Romanov."

"Thank you sir." corporal Romanov said beaming with a smile. "Perhaps we should also alert intropol, I mean the International cops in case they manage to sneak out of the country to Amsterdam."

"I guarantee you they would never leave the shores of this country with their damned cargo Romanov. We will nail them first at the Moscow international airport. God knows those two have dragged the name of Russia in the mud too often. This will be the end of the road for them I guarantee you that!" the superintendent said.

An hour later the two cops left the headquarters for their houses after work looking very happy that evening.

But what corporal Romanov had told his boss was partly right. Masha Alexy and Dima Kisa would be flying to Amsterdam the following week by all means. But what the young corporal perhaps didn't know was that they would be going on Thursday and not on Saturday and Sunday the following week as he had told his senior officer. They would also travel on a Lufthansa aircraft. And they would boldly travel together.

If the cops were to depend on the intelligence reports Romanov had brought there was every likely hood that the pair would have left the country before they can be stopped and searched. If Romanov had his own sources of information, it was likely that Dima Kisa and Masha Alexy had men among the cops who could give misleading information to the cops too.

Somehow the drug barons were still one step ahead of the cops who were bent on getting them.

Some hours later night filled the city. Morning came later and it was Wednesday. Strangly Dimitry Misha's and Maxism Ivanova's lifeless bodies were found at the swimming pool at Dimitry Misha's mansion.

10

DIMA KISA had thought that the death of Maxism Ivanova and Dimitry Misha will bring an end to the search by the cops for the notorious drug peddlers who killed Valodia Ivan, but he was shocked that they still intensified their investigations on the drug peddlers.

At last Thursday night came. The lights at the Moscow international airport made the place look like day. Masha Alexy and Dima Kisa had come to the airport at different times and were about to check their luggage into the Lufthansa aircraft.

Both man and woman did nothing to show the detached bystander that they knew each other.

It was right they did that. Their job called for the strictest secrecy and they had to do what was necessary to maintain that secrecy. Masha Alexy was the tenth person in front of Dima Kisa at the line to check her luggage.

When they got to the customs desk the three officers there asked Masha Alexy if she had anything concealed to declare, she said no.

She looked at the customs man who asked her the routine question. "My body is the only thing I am taking to Amsterdam. Pray however that I come back with money after my business there and I will have a present for each of you," she playfully told the custom officers.

Before long she had been cleared and she went into the long room from where she would not be expected to come out again before she went on board the aircraft.

As she walked through the glass doors into the long room Lady Masha Alexy cast a cursory glance at Dima Kisa who was the tenth person behind her. Everything was going according to plan.

Inside the glass room she looked at Dima Kisa as the customs men also cleared him not aware that the shoe he was wearing had a second sole attached to the original which carried an explosive drug.

As she looked at Dima Kisa she also saw Kolia, arrive in the room and go near Dima Kisa. They did not exchange greetings and did not do anything to show that they knew each other. As Dima Kisa was also cleared into the long room he smiled, went and sat near Masha Alexy.

Kolia had done his job well. The two of them were about to go on board without being stopped. That was the role of a dishonest cop and Masha Alexy would pay him well when they both returned from Holland.

***

Kolia was about to leave the airport and go away when he saw the bodyguard who had driven Dima Kisa to the airport. He signaled to the criminal to stop.

Kolia went near Dima Kisa's car "Didn't your boss give you anything to give to me?" he asked the bodyguard who also was the driver.

"He gave me this parcel containing one thousand dollars to be given to you," the bodyguard replied.

Kolia put one thousand dollars in his jacket pocket and smiled. "I came to the airport to see that nothing happened to him. I gave the cops some misleading information. For all they know he would be traveling next Saturday instead of today. By the time the cops become wise he would have gone to Holland and came back." Kolia said and laughed craftily. "It is surprising to know how stupid the cops in Moscow are. We were smarter at Yakutia before I was brought to the capital."

He turned to go away, but stopped short when he felt a hand on his right arm.

"Now we know who the mysterious Kolia is. We are not so stupid as we know you!" said a voice from behind Kolia. It was the voice of Pushkin. The mysterious Kolia was no other than corporal Romanov the same cop who was second to Pushkin to help trap Dima Kisa.

Corporal Romanov turned around and saw his boss superintendent Pushkin with three armed cops standing behind him.

Pushkin was smiling with satisfaction. Romanov knew he was in a big mess.

"So you are the corrupt cop who had been giving Dima Kisa information about the cop activities?" Pushkin asked as Romanov tried to hide the money he had just received, but it was too late. A cop hand dug into his shirt pocket and took out the money from the envelope. That would be used as evidence against him later in court.

"You think we are stupid here in Moscow, but now you have seen that the stupid one appears to be you," superintendent Pushkin laughed. "We suspected you were a hand in glove with some criminals that is why we brought you from Yakutia to Moscow. And to catch you I deliberately gave you this task of trapping Dima Kisa. At the same time I was watching every step you took. We only wanted to be sure that you were the dishonest cop who was giving all these criminals our secret laid down plan."

There was nothing corporal Romanov could say, there was

nothing to say, he had come to the end of his dishonest career. He looked at his boss superintendent Pushkin, there were a lot of questions on his face that would never get answers. But he had to ask the one question that highly bothered him.

"How did you know I was feeding Dima Kisa information about your efforts to trap him sir?"

"We suspected you especially since we knew of your criminal activities at Yakutia before you got transferred to Moscow. We know that rogue called Dima Kisa was once your brother in law and both of you come from the same country side. We suspected you would not give him up to the law easily."

"I see." corporal Romanov said desperatly.

"But we were not sure of your complicity in the dealings of Dima Kisa who is currently also under arrest for your information. We know all about the drug hidden in the sole of his shoe. Indeed we practically followed him from his house to this place just to trap the two of you."

Corporal Romanov opened his mouth wide in the dark. He was now sure that he was indeed cornered. The one man who could have sprung him from the long arms of the law was himself in the grips of the law. He wondered if Masha Alexy had been arrested as well. The punishment he knew would be coming to him, he tried to help the cops in some way. "There is another woman with Dima Kisa her name is Masha Alexy you have to get her too before she goes on board…"

"Don't worry about that young Lady Masha Alexy whom I first introduced to you. I know you have always wondered about her. Well you don't have to wonder any longer. Indeed she is that reason why you corporal Romanov is going to be behind bars for the rest of your life. If you must know she is not a criminal as I tricked you into believing the first time we saw her at the bank. She is a senior cop officer and a graduate of law if you must know. Even if we had not arrested you taking money from this rogue we would have nailed you all the same."

Corporal Romanov felt his body shivering at the way that

young woman had trapped him. "So she knew all about me the time we met in Dima Kisa's house?"

The armed cops handcuffed Romanov.

"Precisely when you met her at Dima Kisa's residence and she deceived you into believing that she was herself a criminal. You collected some money from her. The following day you deposited some of that money in your bank account. What you did not know was that those notes were secretly marked. So all along we know you corporal Romanov to be the mysterious Kolia who was feeding Dima Kisa all that information on the cops. Even if those notes had not given you out Masha Alexy Nketia would have identified you as the criminal plant. She recorded your entire conversation at Dima Kisa's house with the secret recorder hidden in her skirt button. By the way her real name is not Masha Alexy Nketia as everyone thinks."

Kolia was shocked.

"Are you surprised?"

"Of course yes!" Kolia replied.

"But that is a fact…"

"What is her real name?" corporal Romanov asked knowing that getting to know that name would not help him in any way.

"That I can not tell you maybe when you are behind bars for the rest of your miserable life you can take guesses on that." Pushkin said.

"God I am finished."

"Men haul this criminal and Dima Kisa's driver away!" these last words superintendent Pushkin said to his armed men.

Corporal Romanov was shaking all over now at the prospect of spending the rest of his criminal life in jail with his in law Dima Kisa. There he would have the chance to reflect on how that female cop impostor had tricked the two of them into jail that is if they too are not sentenced to death like the eight that had long been hunged as directed by the court.

The next day the criminals were charged to the court in Moscow. The case lasted for months before a date was fixed for the judgement. The judge had already finished given his judgment before Pushkin's arrival at the court premises that was over crowded with people. He was only to rely on Masha Alexy to get information on the judgement the judge had delivered.

Pushkin began to search for Masha Alexy until he found her discussing the sentence with other cops and he immediately joined them. From a close distance Natasha watched Dima Kisa climb into the Black Maria over whelmed with emotion she managed to pull herself together.

Dima Kisa had stood on the staircase of the Black Maria waving at the crowd with a full smile like a politician on a campaign tour who was sure of victory at the polls. The Russians booed at him and whistling their support to the court judge judgement, but the convicted murderous and blood sucking peddler who once held the nation to ransom kept on waving with a smile. He did not have a reaction of the crowd and continued waving with a toothy smile.

Suddenly his hands hung in the air and his parted smiling lips stood still. His eyes grew larger as if they would jump out of their sockets. Dima Kisa had just sighted Masha Alexy, she looked healthy and hearty. She was being congratulated by the cops' boss, Pushkin and other top Russian government officials.

"Masha Alexy... you lied to me... you told me you are a peddler. Now I know the truth... this woman will live while I die... What a fool I have been!" Dima Kisha lamented before a cop who was an officer took him in and locked the door of the Black Maria. And soon as the lorry weaved through the crowd and headed to the prison yard at kusku, Natasha broke down and wept like a baby.

"What am I living for? My parents are dead and now a man who cares so much about me is going to die... oh! What a world!"

Zhena walked to Natasha and led her into a car and they left the court premises.

With Masha Alexy the great seductive and beautiful female from the Russian cop headquarters in Moscow. The peddlers connection in Russia was broken and broken forever.

www.ingramcontent.com/pod-product-compliance
Lightning Source LLC
Chambersburg PA
CBHW050834180626
46814CB00004B/1618